# Conduits

Jennifer Loring

PUBLICATIONS

Cover by Kealan Patrick Burke, © 2019 LVP
Publications

Conduits Copyright © 2014, 2019 Jennifer Loring

Lycan Valley Press Publications
1625 E 72nd St STE 700 PMB 132
Tacoma, Washington 98404 United States of America

Printed in the United States of America

First LVP Publications Edition, April 2019

ISBN-13: 978-0-9987489-8-6

*For Joe Borrelli*

# THE NOTHING

THE iPHONE TUMBLED from Mara's hand, the voice on the other end distant and metallic, a child talking into a tin can. The ambiguous sense of dread on the bus this morning and now the confirmation of her worst fears. A month had passed since she last spoke to him. His cell phone was shut off, and he'd stopped visiting or going out. All the signs were right in front of her, yet she had done nothing but deny the obvious. Their relationship had been an apt metaphor for his life: over before it truly began.

She reached for the phone, which squeaked, "Hello? Hello? Mara?"

"I'm here."

The sun ducked behind a cloud, and shadows stretched across the floor. The air hung heavy with grief and new ghosts. She had done nothing. Not even when she suspected the worst.

"I... I have to go. Thank you for telling me." She pressed the *end* button and stared at the picture on her bedside table. If she cried, that meant she believed what she had just heard. That he was gone. She felt herself slipping away from her body, as she so often did in times of stress. A gray fuzz like television static descended over her vision, her world.

When she had regained a negligible sense of herself again, Mara wept for two straight weeks.

\* \* \*

**JOURNAL ENTRY:**

*This is what Wikipedia says (I know, what kind of shit journalist uses Wiki as a source?) about the stages of grief:*

DENIAL — Denial is usually only a temporary defense for the individual. It can be conscious or unconscious refusal to accept facts, information, or the reality of the situation. Denial is a defense mechanism, and some people can become locked in this stage.

ANGER — Once in the second stage, the individual recognizes that denial cannot continue. Anger can manifest itself in different ways. People can be angry with themselves, or with others, and especially those who are close to them. It is important to remain detached and nonjudgmental when dealing with a person experiencing anger from grief.

BARGAINING — The third stage involves the hope that the individual can somehow postpone or delay death. Usually, the negotiation for an extended life is made with a higher power in exchange for a reformed lifestyle. Bargaining rarely provides a sustainable solution, especially if it's a matter of life or death.

*The pain becomes a maze, and through the maze echoes the words, "If only..." and "What if..." What if I had one more chance to say what I should have?*

\* \* \*

"You can't think like this, Mara. It's not healthy."

"You're not supposed to try talking me out of my feelings. I read about it."

"You read too much."

Only someone who hated reading would say something so stupid. It was moments like these that Mara questioned whether she and Andrea knew each other at all.

Andrea scrunched her freckled nose. "Maybe your parents were right. Maybe you should go to Japan for a while. I mean, especially if they're paying. You can still write while you're there."

Her parents rarely called. Though they'd lived in this country most of their lives, they believed America had "ruined" her—anything for assurance that the blame did not lie with them. Shame culture was alive and well in the Okubo family. "They're paying because they feel guilty. They hated Jason."

"They never even met him."

Mara laughed. Nothing had ever sounded so hollow, so utterly false. "They didn't need to know him. He was in a band and on drugs. Case closed. They'd love me to go to Japan and fall in love with a rich businessman. Who, with my luck, would commit suicide within a year."

"Mara, I'm worried about you. Maybe you need to, you know… talk to someone."

"A therapist." She picked at a piece of lint on her hoodie. What did Andrea know? She had a perfect job, a perfect boyfriend… Soon enough she'd leave too, sticking Mara with rent on a house she couldn't afford as she clawed her way up the ladder at the magazine.

*Misplaced feelings of rage and envy.* Back to stage two. She'd read every goddamned printed word on grief at this point. The knowledge she gleaned only sharpened the pain, focused it into a beam like a gamma ray burst exploding through her universe. If only it would finish the job and annihilate her completely. "I don't know. Maybe."

"Listen. I'll try to be here more. We'll do stuff like we used to." Andrea clasped Mara's hands. "We all loved Jason. And I can't imagine how hard this is for you. Think about taking your parents up on their offer, okay?"

"Yeah. I'll think about it."

"Great. Let's order takeout, and watch a bad movie."

Mara forced a smile. "Thanks, Andrea."

"Any time." Andrea hugged her. "I know it doesn't feel like it right now, but it's going to get better. I promise."

*You can't promise what is not in your power to give.* But Mara returned her roommate's embrace, if only in the hope Andrea would end the discussion.

\* \* \*

Glass. She didn't know why she preferred glass to a razor blade, or a knife, or even a pin. It was more difficult to find a piece not potentially contaminated with something just lying around, and that made it all the more special. This was pain they could control, she with her glass and he with his drugs. No longer were they passive recipients; they dictated where and when and how much and for how long. When she needed to slip out of her own skin, needed an endorphin rush, she would find a bathroom or a dark hallway. Anywhere that might shield her from the disapproving eyes of those who believed she ought to suck up whatever life threw at her, but had no right to pain on her own terms. She would slip the cold sliver into her hand, and cut the inside of her arm or thigh, an area no one could see with her clothing in place, deep enough for the beautiful red bubbles to rise to the surface.

Mara sat on the bathroom floor and locked the door just in case Andrea returned sooner than expected. The cold of the tiles was a sensation like the glass, a sharp cut reminding her she was still alive. She held the bloodstained shard between her thumb and index finger, scraping it along the pale flesh of her inner thigh. A thin line like a fingernail scratch, except for the crimson globules her glass awakened, and with the blood she could breathe again, could pretend for a little while longer that she would be all right. Mara pressed a fresh tissue to the wound, imprinting upon it a pattern she would try to decipher later, perhaps, once she taped it and locked it safely away in her journal. When so little else seemed to have meaning anymore, she hoped to find some within herself.

\* \* \*

"Sleep has its own world," Byron once wrote. Mara, lying in bed after spicy Thai food that made her stomach gurgle, fell asleep in her Seattle apartment and awoke in a dark forest ribboned with mist.

Distant bells chimed in an eerie rhythm that reminded her of her grandfather. Whenever they had visited him in Japan, they attended ceremonies at the local Shinto shrine; what drifted through the forest sounded like the handheld *Suzu* used in those rituals. She felt strangely linked by their resonance to her ancestors, though she did not often think of herself as Japanese at all. She was an American girl through and through, much to her parents' chagrin, and they had urged her more than once to spend some time in Japan, reconnect with her culture in a way they could not provide. More than once, she had come within hours of booking a flight. But she always found a class she needed to take or, after graduation, a promising assignment she believed would make her career, catapulting her to instant success.

Then she'd met Jason.

*There should be a crescent moon,* she thought. But the sky was smooth, starless black velvet. A blanket smothering the world.

He had stopped breathing as soon as he lay down. They found him dead in his room the next morning. Didn't drink more than usual or take anything he hadn't ingested a million times. Just happened to take the wrong combination of the two. For all the sorrow it brought, his death surprised no one. A rock 'n' roll cliché. A minor footnote in local music history.

If only that made it hurt less.

Mara followed both the sound of the bells and what resembled a path. The edges of her vision flickered with pale shapes flitting through the trees. Whether they were leading her or stalking her, she couldn't tell. She hadn't been here long enough to be afraid, and given that she'd never before experienced lucid dreaming, she was more fascinated than frightened. She was certain, however, that she was not alone.

The branches parted to reveal a thin black stripe woven into the forest floor—a river with tiny guttering forms floating on the surface as both wended their way deeper into the night. Candles within paper lanterns. The souls of the dead.

The bells; she could only hear the bells—no chatter of birds or insects, whatever nocturnal animals typically dwelled in forests. Even the water itself flowed in majestic silence, magnifying the eerie beauty of the lanterns upon its surface. Mara knelt beside the river and dipped her fingers into the dark liquid. The abysmal iciness numbed her hand, and she quickly pulled away. Nothing was colder than death. Except, perhaps, love.

Mara continued down the path, beside the river, as the trees thinned out. Sharp mountain peaks loomed behind whatever lay in the clearing just beyond the trees, guardians of this soundless world. *Kunitsu-kami* inhabited these trees, those mountains, even the river. A world full of spirits, the universe's interconnecting energy. A parallel, invisible world.

Most of the time.

The bells grew louder in proportion to the woods' retreat. In a few moments, Mara stood before an estate too massive to be possible, with wings, additions, and outbuildings arranged in a haphazard fashion. Snow began to fall.

And Jason waiting on the top step, his hand around the doorknob. He turned toward her, as white as the snow fluttering around him, his every gesture as languid as slow-motion video. He waved to her.

"Jason," Mara screamed, the reverberations tearing through her throat, yet no sound emerging from her mouth. The bells, the maddening, deafening bells...

Jason smiled, flickered like the lanterns, and vanished into the house.

* * *

Mara gasped and swiped at the tears on her cheeks. Stripes of wan orange streetlight painted the ceiling and wall. The dead lingered in the darkness at the far end of the room, the ephemera of a fading dream.

*Just a dream.* Jason saying good-bye. That might be enough to get her through the rest of the night. She was exhausted, after all. Between work and

Jason's death, she'd been hanging by a thread for weeks. Andrea's concerns held some validity; her emotional state limped along on life support.

Mara closed her eyes. She'd do something about it, but she wouldn't go to Japan. She wouldn't give her parents the satisfaction. They wanted her to forget he'd ever existed.

\* \* \*

**JOURNAL ENTRY:**

*In dream symbology, snow represents cleansing and purity. A mansion represents the mind, body, and spirit of a person.*

*But which one of us? Is he in my mansion?*

*Or have I found a way into his? Is dreaming the way back to him?*

\* \* \*

Mara set her journal on the edge of the sink and sank into a bubble bath, a luxury she rarely had time to indulge anymore. She imagined the foamy peaks as snowcapped mountains. Her legs grew heavy with the weight of the water, and she closed her eyes. When she opened them again, a tiny black speck of fuzz tainted the perfect, fluffy whiteness. That one little dot enough to ruin the entire bath.

Mara began to cry, and though she wanted to climb out of the tub, she stayed until her hands and feet pruned, until the last bubble melted away into the tepid water.

She dragged herself out of the tub, slipped into her warmest pajamas, and, with the journal tucked under her arm, wandered downstairs into the kitchen. Rain, the city's most famous feature, sluiced over the windows. Behind the blinds, it resembled long, emaciated fingers reaching down from the roof. Mara hated being alone in the house. Despite the modern design, it was too dark, even with all the lights on. She wished they had a cat, regardless of the animal's notorious penchant for indifference. It would have been another living creature in the house with her. Andrea had gone… somewhere. Was it her and Nick's anniversary today?

Mara leaned against the breakfast bar, whose pass-through overlooked the living room. At only seven thirty, wan light filtered through the curtains like the first dusk after the end of the world. The house took on the grainy texture of an archaic film. Mara shivered. She wanted to get her robe, but as she eyed the darkened staircase, she decided against it.

"You're a grown woman," she chastised herself. "Stop being pathetic."

She couldn't see the TV from this angle, but the hiss of the set tuned to a dead channel caught her attention. She constantly had to remind Andrea to turn it off. Mara walked into the living room and picked up the remote but did not press the button. One could pick out strange patterns if they studied the screen for even a few minutes. A Rorschach of electromagnetic waves, nothing more than pareidolia data despite their determination to resolve into faces, into whispers. Raudive voices riding the electronic spectrum. And if she stared long enough, she could almost see…

*Not that. Please, not that.*

Rain beat harder against the glass, an intruder demanding entrance. The curtains shifted in a breeze that could not have come from the closed window.

*They did* not; *quit scaring yourself—*

Her phone chimed, and she nearly tripped over her own feet, half-terrified and half-relieved at the familiar sound. She reached over one of the bar chairs to snatch it off the counter, her legs two balloons full of warm water. Maybe Andrea, inviting her to be the pitiable third wheel on an evening when she should be thinking of no one but Nick.

"Hello?"

Static, like the susurrating TV. A faint jingle of *Suzu.* Beads of sweat popped out on her forehead and upper lip.

"Hello? Who's there? Answer me!"

*…you will know it is time…*

*When I was little, little, little,*

*I played, played, played—*

Mara pressed "end" with such force she thought she'd cracked the screen. She let the phone tumble onto the carpet. Silence. Unnerving, deafening. The warm air teemed with the invisible dead, with their dreams and memories. Their pain.

*I won't do this again. I won't go crazy again.*

Mara rushed into the half-bath down the hall, fleeing the darkness closing in behind her. If she looked back, she knew she would see something she didn't want to, something that shouldn't be there. Mara slammed the door shut and locked it. She picked up the hairbrush beside the sink and rammed the handle's blunt end into the bottom of the mirror until the glass splintered, and she could pluck a shard from its remains. She pulled down her pajama bottoms, then sat on the toilet lid, and, with quaking hands, scraped at her skin until the blood came and she could breathe again.

\* \* \*

"How does this look?"

Mara studied the sketch stenciled onto her left thigh. He loved roses. At least a dozen flash designs of that flower adorned the shop's walls, but Mara had scoured the Internet for the perfect representation of their love: a white rose spattered with blood. The petals like his skin, absorbing the only thing of value she possessed. Drinking in the life she wished she could have given for his.

"Perfect."

"Awesome. Come on back and have a seat."

Mara settled into a chair as the artist snapped on a fresh pair of latex gloves and opened a package of needles. He filled little cups with various ink colors.

"First tattoo?"

"Yeah."

"It shouldn't hurt too much where you're getting it. The more skin, the better. You'll probably feel something like being snapped by a rubber band over and over."

That, she thought, would hardly be an issue. Without a doubt, he would see the scars, like tiny pale grubs feeding on her flesh.

"So, what made you want to get this one?"

Mara winced as the gun punched into her thigh. "I lost someone recently."

"Ah. Sorry to hear that. But this is a great way to remember them, you know? They'll be with you forever."

Pain, like snow, cleansed and purified. Mara welcomed the blood, the needles that stung like a thousand wasps in her leg. In this rose, in this scarlet torment, he was hers for eternity. She wouldn't have to cut today. Maybe not ever again.

"That's the idea." She smiled as the artist swabbed away the blood welling up from her newly colored flesh.

* * *

Andrea crinkled her nose as she always did when expressing disapproval. "I like tattoos as much as the next girl, but… maybe you weren't in the best frame of mind to get one just yet."

Mara frowned and twisted her leg so she could see the tattoo. It was the most beautiful artwork ever applied to a human body. "What's wrong with it?"

"Nothing. I mean, technically it's amazing. But it's just a little… creepy. I don't know. The blood, I guess. It's a little… morbid." Andrea shrugged. "Hey, it's your body. Listen, Nick has a friend who's a photographer, and he's gone out to the forest around Mount Rainier a few times to shoot. You know that house in the woods everyone always talks about? Turns out it may have been the base of operations for some cult a couple years back. Ritual sacrifice and everything."

Mara sat in the vintage armchair she'd picked up at a thrift store. People were so quick to throw out what wasn't new enough or cool enough. She, on the other hand, had always been compelled to rescue things, to fix them. It was what had drawn her to Jason. She was nothing if not a glutton for punishment, a masochist of the highest order. "The house where people still go missing, right?"

"That's the one. We can drive out this weekend if you want to take a look. I know how much you like that stuff, and you could write about it. I mean… if it's not too soon." Andrea shook her head suddenly and slashed the air with one hand, slicing through the offer hanging in the air. "Forget it. It's not the best time…"

Mara hadn't been interested in writing, or life in general, for weeks. Only cutting. Only getting the excruciating pain out of her. But the paranormal had fascinated her since she was a little girl. Probably her grandfather's doing, with his stories of ghost-and demon-haunted Japan. Each year until his death, she had eagerly awaited her family's annual summer vacation to his rural village. But something about his house, a large traditional with tatami mats and sliding doors, had terrified her. She supposed that was what lured her to these so-called haunted houses—an attempt to exorcise the old fear, prove she'd never had reason to be afraid. A dark tourist confronting the terrors of her own childhood.

The dreams and Andrea's proposition were, naturally, mere coincidence.

Mara considered telling her what she had experienced last night, but feared it was too easy to dismiss as another manifestation of her grief. Like poltergeist phenomena, or spontaneous psychokinesis. ("Psychosis" made a brief infringement into her thoughts, but she refused to acknowledge its presence.) It would make a great article, actually, once she marshaled the strength to write about her own pain, or anything else for that matter. If ever.

"Let's do it."

Andrea clapped, her eyes sparkling. She thought Mara was coming out of it, of course. She thought she was taking Mara's mind off Jason. She had no idea Jason was the reason for the trip.

"I'll set it up for Saturday. This will do you good. You've been sleeping too much. Maybe you'll get some ideas for that book you wanted to write."

Mara swallowed hard and stared at the fingers she laced and unlaced. Jason had been her biggest cheerleader, her fearless supporter when the rest of the world laughed and assured her she'd never make it. He had heard it all himself.

She would write the goddamned book. She'd write it for both of them.

\* \* \*

Raining again. Always raining. She looked out the window and traced the fingers of water gliding down the glass like God's tears. So much sadness. So much suffering. No wonder it rained all the time.

*And when I was dead, dead, dead,*
*I was scared, scared, scared...*

"Mara?"

She turned. Something cold swept past her as Andrea walked around the kitchen bar and into the living room. But Andrea's expression disclosed no fear, no admission that she, too, had experienced the anomalous breeze. Only the sort of distress seen in the faces of relatives newly informed that their loved one was hopelessly, untreatably insane.

*You don't understand, Andrea,* she wanted to say. *I had a dream… and I think something came back with me.*

"Mara… what are you doing?"

"Just looking out the window," she said, but her own voice sounded unreal to her, not her own. The film grain texture cast a permanent filter over her vision. She was trapped in someone else's world, or they in hers. So many pieces already missing for the puzzle of her life, and now someone had picked it up, leaving her helpless to do anything but watch the remaining fragments disengage from each other and tumble away. Panic sapped the strength from her body.

"You were singing. Are you okay? Maybe we should go out for a while. I'm starting to think that trip this weekend is a bad idea, too."

"Is there something… standing next to me?"

Andrea's face drained of color. "What are you talking about? You're scaring me, Mara."

"Please don't leave me here alone," Mara whispered. Her eyes dimmed with tears, and she was glad, because she didn't want to see anymore.

\* \* \*

## JOURNAL ENTRY:

*It's a sunny day as we drive toward the mountain. The kind of day where nothing bad could ever happen, because it's just too beautiful.*

*Lately I've been thinking about all the theories of paranormal activity. So much of it centers on electrical energy. What happens to that energy when we die? First Law of Thermodynamics. If it can't be destroyed, it must change into... something.*

*I've dreamed about him every night. I did some more research about the forest and the general area where the house is supposed to be. There are so many urban legends. They say there are orbs, strange voices, the usual stuff you can see any night on the SyFy Channel. This went on even before the alleged cult activity. I read that kids dare each other to come out here. Some never come back. I didn't have time to check any of the missing person reports, but it's the first thing I plan to do when I get home.*

*Because I have to know. I have to know why I'm seeing him in the forest, why this place. Why everything feels so completely wrong, and why I feel like the dead are closing in around me.*

*I don't want Andrea to be right. I don't want to be crazy.*

\* \* \*

"I heard the Indians own it," Andrea said from the front seat, "but they all left because it's haunted."

"Let me guess—a sacred burial ground? Come on, Andi." Nick laughed as he drove down a gravel road. "It's a bunch of trees." He caught Mara's eye in the rearview mirror, smiled, and shook his head. She closed the journal and tucked it into her bag. "Welcome to paradise, ladies."

"You're an ass." Andrea folded her arms and refused to budge from the passenger seat until he opened the door. She had tried to talk Mara out of coming last night, and again this morning. *It was a stupid idea. I don't think you're ready. Let's just hang out.* "You came here with Chris. Where's the path?"

"Relax. It's right behind those trees."

Mara fixed her gaze on the spot where Nick pointed. She thought she heard, so distant she could almost dismiss it, the chiming of *Suzu*. But it was enough to propel her forward into the darkness within the forest.

"Come on," she said with a wave of her hand. "Follow me."

The trees seemed to interlock their branches over the path, an impenetrable fence over which she could not climb, through which she could not cut. The road was invisible to her. The trail crunched with leaves and twigs after years of disuse. Sunlight flickered between branches creating patterns and shadows in the wood that, from the corner of her eye, appeared to move.

*Like lanterns…*

She walked a short time before glancing over her shoulder to make sure Nick and Andrea still followed. "Andrea?"

Both Andrea and Nick, in just a few minutes' time, had vanished.

*They're screwing with you. They probably ran off to make out somewhere.*

She scanned the trees for signs of movement, strained to hear Andrea's familiar giggle. But the unnatural silence burrowed with termite insistence into Mara's bones, and she shuddered with an involuntary chill despite the sweat dribbling down the back of her neck. A thousand invisible eyes stared at her from the trees, the atmosphere thick with unseen bodies. Her fingers clenched and unclenched with need.

Then, once again, the faint siren's call of jingling *Suzu*.

"I'm heading up the path," she shouted to break the spell. "Catch up with me!"

The trees thinned out a short distance ahead. Beneath Mara's feet, the dirt trail turned into flagstones shattered by weeds. On either side stood small stones at regular intervals, with dead flowers strewn about their bases. She had seen many outside rural Japanese villages. *Dōsojin*, she recalled.

Protectors meant to safeguard travelers against evil spirits.

A twelve-foot metal gate erupted from the earth, so entwined with weeds and branches that it had become a part of the forest itself. Mara rattled the metal red with rust. The gate wasn't locked, but the twining vegetation had sealed it shut. She stepped back to snap a few pictures. Beyond the tangle of trees lay the one- and two-story shapes of semi-ruined buildings, defenders of the massive structure lying deeper within the wood. Their empty windows peered blindly at her like eyeless sockets.

Mara lowered the phone. Someone had made a hole in the fence just large enough for a crouching person to wriggle through. Probably those teenagers, maybe one who had never returned. She pushed the chain link out of her way and, hunching over, breached the fence. A sharp, broken metal link snagged on her arm. Mara hissed, snatched her arm away, and clapped her hand over the wound. *How is this any different from what you do to yourself?* they would ask, though the answer was obvious.

"Shit," she muttered as she lifted her hand. A few drops of blood pattered onto the forest floor, and more smeared her palm. Mara wiped it on her jeans, then shuffled through the contents of her bag for her little plastic bandage case. She smoothed the Band-Aid onto her arm. The pad darkened with blood.

"Great start to this adventure." She sighed and

picked her way along something that resembled a sidewalk, albeit one on the losing end of a jackhammer. A chill washed over her despite the increasing heat, and she shivered. The air thickened with humidity and with the sensation of a hundred bodies crowding in around her. Mara caught her breath.

*Just my imagination. Which has been on overdrive lately.*

She focused instead on the outbuildings. She'd never have time to investigate all of them, let alone whatever lie within the trees beyond. But there was no river. It couldn't be the house from her dream.

*I still need to see it. I don't know why, but I do.*

She pushed ahead, and the weeds closed in again as if to hide a terrible secret. If the rumors were true, ghosts haunted every leaf and pebble of this forest. Natives had come here centuries ago on spirit quests and fled in terror from whatever they found.

The main building, a crumbling wreck of bricks, shingles, and wood constructed of pure misery, its foundation obscured by grasses so dense it seemed the forest itself had fashioned it, emerged from the overgrowth. Nothing—

No one, she corrected herself; *things* did not build

—

—happy or even remotely sane would have created such a monstrosity. Prisons were more inviting than this, an edifice whose façade of shattered windows and broken doors resembled nothing so much as a demonic face glowering at anyone who dared intrude upon its domain. Even worse, the chaotic additions plunged into the forest like tentacles, or climbed into the sky as if entreating God to relieve whatever plagued its builder's damaged mind.

Mara snapped several more photos. She stood in what must have been a courtyard, though only one statue remained—the figure of a woman who, by accident or design, possessed no head. She thumbed through the phone's camera roll. Great shots for the urban exploration site she frequented, but nothing out of the ordinary.

She flipped back one frame. A white blur in the second-story window. Mara zoomed in until the smudge filled the entire screen.

Dark spaces delineated what should have been features, but it was undoubtedly a face. A human face, the color of skin on vanilla pudding. A face that, somehow, stirred up a sickly feeling of déjà vu.

Her hands trembling, Mara whispered into the voice recorder on her phone, "I've found... something. A building. It's huge. And I caught something on camera, looking out the window. I won't get through much today, but I'm going inside."

Mara mounted the decrepit concrete steps, the first of which had almost completely dissolved into the grass but for a crooked chunk perhaps six inches long. Remnants of white paint clung to the wooden front doors like the last shreds of hope. Mara tugged on a curved brass handle, and the door clattered within its frame but refused her entry. Her heartbeat ticked away the seconds. If she didn't get in soon, she'd have to turn back.

Mara scooted over to one of the tall, low windows. She used her bag to smash out the remaining fangs of glass, then brushed them off the sill and into the weeds. She tossed the bag through the window before hoisting herself up and trailing it into the building. Mara retrieved the bag and fumbled in the darkness for her phone and the flashlight app. Shielded by trees, the windows did not readily admit sunlight. A sense of foreboding merged with the disconcerting idea that she had arrived exactly where she belonged. Even the air embraced her with unexpected warmth. She'd seen enough photos of abandoned buildings to expect the graffiti on the walls, its very existence bragging of the artists' (and she used that term loosely —"Mike T. sucks cock" was hardly the pinnacle of Western civilization) bravery. Unopened boxes were stacked in one corner, tempting Mara to discover what the house's occupants so hastily abandoned, but it would have to wait for another trip.

In the shifting light, penumbral forms slipped down the hallway, away from her beam. Optical illusions, just like the thing in the window. Seeing what she wanted to see, because if there were no such things as ghosts, then she had to accept that she really *was* crazy.

Mara entered the hall and, peering into a doorway, swept the light across the room. Paint peeled from the walls like a bad sunburn, and moth-eaten lace curtains fluttered in a spectral breeze, despite the stifling lack of air circulation. Someone's attempt at sprucing up the place. Either a kind gesture or a cruel joke, depending on the house's original purpose, though it appeared harmless enough despite the odd location. A mattress, without a frame or box spring and stained with water or mold—or blood—slumped in one corner. The depth of decay overpowered her; each mote of dust intended to suffocate her with whatever anguish transpired here. And she was convinced it had. Every molecule laden with suffering, with some appalling misery into which she had willingly meddled. Her own sorrow so fresh, her mind so hypersensitive, she was a circuit through which others might transmit their grief. Something wished to do so, or it would not have gazed down at her from that window. It would not have called to her in her dreams and used Jason as bait.

She turned her light to the room across the hall. Here the paint on the wall was crisp, black, like barbecued flesh. A fire, though neither the rest of the room nor the hall bore similar scorch marks. She flashed the beam to the other wall.

Handprints. Bloody—

*"When you hear the singing, you will know it is time."*

Mara whirled around, her stomach in her throat.

"Who's there?" she called. She scratched her thigh, where beneath the denim her skin flaked as it healed. "Answer me!"

But no one did, and when she turned back to the room, nothing marred the paint but bald patches where time and neglect had taken their toll. Mara crept back toward the entrance. Shadows thronged together, black as an oil slick rippling above the water. All life ensnared in its darkness, unable to breathe, unable to escape. Lungs filling with the greasy blackness—

Mara sucked in as deep a breath as she could hold. Her wrists and neck burned. God, the air in here... she had to get out.

She thought she heard the faintest echo of water, like a stream flowing through a cave. Above her, the ceiling groaned with the despair of decades. Dust and lead paint filtered into her hair. She raised her flashlight beam to the debris drifting down. A curve of shoulder, the suggestion of a head, determined to coalesce into an actual form. The creaking sound slithered down the wall behind her. Mara spun around. Had the paint bubbled just now?

The door is right there. Get out—

She took a step toward the door. The flashlight illuminated a deadbolt so rusted she doubted she could twist it open. Still she reached for it, the metal inexplicably frigid against her fingers, and jiggled the lock. The floorboards whined behind her. She'd have to go back through the window. Her heart thumped in her ears as Mara tossed her bag into the weeds outside. Sunlight warmed her arms, her hands, a beacon leading her to the safety, the normality, of the world outside.

She looked back once, despite the churning in her stomach. She had conjured these phantoms in her head, easy enough to do in a fertile atmosphere like this.

The floorboards stopped their moaning. Mara directed the light at them, expecting to see the black button eyes of a rat, or a hairless pink tail slinking back into the darkness.

*You crossed the river,* said a voice, and she wasn't sure if it had come from somewhere in the house or from her own mouth. Either way, the rivers were miles from here.

The eyes were black indeed, but they stared at her with the sort of malice prevalent in only one species. And when long, pale fingers crawled out from beneath the planks, Mara's body rendered itself immobile. The window might as well have been light years away. She thought of the statue in the courtyard and wondered if she was the next addition to that Medusa's garden. Would Andrea and Nick come looking for her? Would they know *where* to search?

When the thing beneath the floorboards hooked its fingernails into the wood and dragged itself out of its hiding place, Mara screamed until all the light in the world went out.

* * *

It was dark when Mara awoke, and a high tide of relief swept over her to find herself in bed. She reached for her bedside lamp but found only empty space. As her eyes adjusted, she realized the room was not merely unfamiliar but *wrong*. Its angles mirrored those of her bedroom, yet the closet, its door ajar—

*I never leave the door open.*

—stood where the window ought to be, and that window clad in ancient lace curtains…

Andrea sat on the edge of the bed and switched on the lamp, on the opposite side from where Mara had left it. The disorientation that came after emerging from a particularly vivid dream, the sense that the world in which one had awakened was not the correct one, normally passed within seconds. Mara, however, could not shake the temporal and spatial dissonance this time. Erratic quantum particles splitting the universe in two, and she'd woken in the wrong one. A balloon of dread expanded in her chest.

Andrea smiled down at her, but it too was wrong. Too toothy, like something unaccustomed to the mechanisms of the human face. A mask.

"You really gave us a scare," Andrea said. Mara hoped this imposter would not touch her, lest its unreality contaminate her. "These nightmares you've been having!"

"I keep seeing Jason. Every night."

Andrea scrunched up her face. It was not the endearing expression of displeasure to which Mara was accustomed, but a monstrous approximation of human emotion rendered by the alien thing beneath Andrea's skin.

"Mara... who is Jason?" She gawped at Mara with fishlike stupidity.

The question sucker punched her. This was cruel, and Andrea was not given to cruelty. To pretend he didn't exist—was this her new tactic to preserve Mara's sanity, by making her question it? Some quack New Age anti-psychiatry bullshit?

They had read the obituary together. And Mara a hundred times after that. Jason Marsico. Beloved son of. Survived by. No mention of her, of course. She was just the flavor of the month; give him a couple weeks and he'd be on to the next. I love you, baby, but it's getting too intense. You'll always be my girl. And when the party ended on that terrible morning after the phone call, she was the beaten and emptied piñata at a child's birthday party. She was the garbage in the Pacific gyre. The Nothing.

"Andrea, that's sick. Why would you even say that?"

Andrea did not respond. Mara sighed and leaned back against her pillows. She scratched absently at her thigh. She wanted to cut.

"Get out," she said, and closed her eyes.

# COMMITTED

ANDREA WAS PERCHED in a chair across from Mara's bed. No, not *her* bed. A hospital bed. Mara clutched at the thin cotton gown that replaced her clothes. A plastic band circled her wrist. No door, just a curtain, left open. The emergency room.

"What the fuck…"

"I'm so sorry, Mara. I didn't know what else to do. They're waiting for a bed to open upstairs, and they'll only keep you for seventy-two hours, unless…"

"You had me *committed?*"

Andrea winced. "For your own safety. The things you say… they don't make any sense. And you're seeing things."

"I'm *dreaming*," Mara growled.

"Besides, I found these." Andrea gestured at a small leather-bound book and a rust-stained glass fragment on her lap. Mara's stomach pitched, and acid seared its way into her throat. She'd have felt less violated if Andrea had raped her.

"Give me those!"

Andrea shook her head. "I think it's best if the doctor takes a look at these. Why couldn't you tell me you were hurting yourself?"

What a stupid question. Mara enfolded her arms, her only remaining armor, around herself. "How did I get here?"

"You keep talking about ghosts. And a house—"

"The house. Is that where you found me?"

"What house? Mara—" Andrea reached for her hand, but Mara slapped it away. Andrea's face darkened. "You shouldn't do that, Mara. Not here."

"Why not? Are you going to tell them to keep me longer? You wanted me gone anyway, so you and Nick could move in together—"

"I better go." Andrea slung her purse over her shoulder. "I would've brought some of your clothes, but they probably won't let you have them anyway." She stopped in the space between the room and the hallway. The squeak of soft-soled shoes against the tile floor, the hum of utterly banal conversations between nurses about their lunch selections and their children's extracurricular activities, the occasional groan of pain... Mara would go crazy here. How could she solve the mystery of what had happened to her if she couldn't shut off these channels competing for her attention?

"I hope things get better for you, Mara. I'll call

your parents and have them get your stuff."

"I knew it. You conniving bitch! Why are you doing this to me? What about Jason?"

Andrea lowered her gaze and shook her head. "Good luck, Mara."

Mara stared after her. The solemn tick of the clock began a long countdown of involuntary incarceration. She wasn't crazy. She hadn't imagined any of it. But how easily Andrea had deceived her with an intricate plot years in the making, each lie so thoroughly rehearsed that Mara had never noticed the threads. Had she snagged just one, she might have unraveled the entire scheme.

Mara drifted in and out of sleep. No one checked on her for a very long time. She shivered beneath the cheap institutional blanket and invented murderous scenarios for Andrea's demise.

*Oh, please. If you kill anyone, it'll be yourself. And that's why you're really here.*

But Andrea… The Andrea Mara knew would not abandon her suicidally depressed friend to a psych ward. She wouldn't give up on her.

The dissonance beset her again. A rip existed somewhere in the fabric of space and time, and she had fallen through into a ghastly parallel universe. She peeked under the blanket and lifted the hem of her gown, a faded rag that had seen hundreds of washings. All the bacteria and viruses it must have encountered made her want to crawl out of her skin. Bacteria were notoriously hard to kill. Even now, they could be colonizing her.

Or, she thought with a terrifying, insect calm, she could simply slice her skin off altogether. Like peeling away a giant scab.

She pushed the thought away and studied her tattoo. It had healed perfectly, the rose a blinding white spattered with lifelike droplets of blood. It still itched, though. When she succumbed to scratching it, her fingernails left four deep crimson furrows in her flesh, as if she'd scraped away the skin with a shard of glass.

\* \* \*

Later that night, two orderlies escorted Mara in a wheelchair, though she was perfectly capable of walking, to the seventh floor. The unit contained only fourteen beds. She overheard the suggestion from a nurse that they move her to Harborview, the actual mental hospital, if her case proved as severe as her friend claimed.

Her official introduction to the ward involved an invasive prodding of every orifice by cold, gloved fingers, lest she hide any contraband that might aid in her only means of-escape. They couldn't possibly grant her that kind of autonomy, to take her own life. In her state of mind, she couldn't possibly know what was best for her.

*They do the same thing to new inmates in prison. They can pretend all they want that this is different.*

Mara bit her lip. She wondered if the nurse, or

whatever function her examiner served, admired her tattoo. No matter how beautiful it was, they wouldn't admit to sharing a similar aesthetic with a mental patient. From there it was a slippery slope to finding themselves on the other side of the gloves.

"Put your gown back on," said the examiner, "and follow me."

With paper slippers on her feet, Mara shuffled behind the nurse to an equally cold, windowless room. She ought to savor these last moments of privacy. She'd done this before, and that fact worried her as she sat down for her intake interview. They'd use it against her to transfer her to Harborview long-term.

The head nurse was exactly the sort of woman Mara expected: fat, her mouth a grim slash between plump cheeks, her eyes flecks of steel that had seen more than their share of sadness and, compassion-fatigued, could no longer be bothered to give a damn.

"This is a dream, isn't it?"

The nurse's lips became a thin pink rind as she flipped through Mara's chart. "You spent an extended period at Harborview ten years ago."

She had put the incident out of her mind for so many years. An impressive feat, all things considered, but it was the only way to maintain any shred of sanity. Of course the staff would bring it up. They needed her to be crazy; otherwise, they had no justifications for keeping her. And Joby was just the ticket. "I found my sister's body. You might snap a little, too."

An almost imperceptible scowl dimmed the nurse's expression even further. Did she think Mara lied? That was what crazy people did, wasn't it—made things up? "I understand your"—the nurse scanned the page—"boyfriend died recently. You appear to be susceptible to triggering events. Have you been experiencing symptoms since your release from Harborview, or only since your recent loss?"

"I'm not sure what you mean by 'symptoms.' The woman who admitted me—Andrea—she set me up—" Mara clamped her mouth shut. She stared at the nurse's pen strokes. She could see it now: *Self-mutilation. Paranoia. Persistent delusions. Possible hallucinations.*

"Ms. Okubo, we want to help you—"

"You think I'm schizophrenic, don't you?"

"—but you need to cooperate with us."

"In what way am I not cooperating? Do you really think I want to be here?"

"I'll take you to your room now." The nurse rose from the table and tucked Mara's file under her arm.

"Are you keeping me in maximum? I haven't done anything."

"Given your history, we will keep you in this ward, for your own safety and others', until we've assessed your behavior. Only the doctor can determine whether you're suited to the minimum security ward."

"When do I see him?"

"Within seventy-two hours. Follow me, please."

Three *days*? She didn't have that kind of time.

The nurse led her to a drab room with pale blue walls. Her roommate, a girl little more than stretched paper across a frame of bones, lay in the bed beneath the barred window. Surely, she was no danger to anyone but herself, and even then, it was the most passive death imaginable. Growing smaller and smaller until she simply evaporated from the world, until she became the ghost she already resembled, hollow-eyed and nearly transparent. But there was that forbidden self-determination again. She would eat what they told her to, and she would go back out into the world to suffer and die like a normal person. Accepting death was healthy. Choosing it... well, that was pure madness. Allowing anyone that kind of freedom was a danger they could not risk. Others might start wanting the same thing.

The doors never closed in this ward, not until lights out and the nurses locked everyone inside. Mara climbed onto her bed and curled her legs under herself.

"Hi," she said. "I'm Mara."

"I know." The girl's phantom voice was so thin Mara thought she imagined it. She turned toward the wall. Her gown revealed tent-pole arms and legs devoid of flesh but for the thin white tube of skin binding her together. Mara was glad she could no longer see the death mask of her face. She switched on her bedside lamp, a hotel-style light drilled securely into the wall above her, the bulb fully enclosed in a metal cage so she couldn't smash it and slash her wrists.

*Aching aching I need to get the pain out need to cut need...*

Mara looked again at her roommate. A network of scarlet lacerations traced the same paths as her veins down her legs, arms, even the back of her neck.

"Jesus," Mara whispered.

"I've seen you in my dreams."

"That's not possible." Mara rubbed her thigh. She rolled up the hem of her gown, just barely above her knee. Her heart punched its way out of her chest and into her throat.

An elaborate tangle of abrasions embraced the entirety of her upper leg. With each thump of her pulse, the gashes squeezed like a metal cilice and intensified in color, staking their claim on her for whatever darkness they served.

"You crossed the river. You can't go back now; they won't let you. They've tasted your life."

"Crossed what river?" Mara wanted to scream. Someone—maybe Andrea—had deprived her of some vital knowledge, and she'd never get out of this if she could not uncover its source.

She needed her journal back. If she wrote it all down, she might discover patterns and clues she had previously overlooked. She was a writer, after all, even in here. And the story of a lifetime was unfolding right before her eyes.

* * *

The lethargy that nailed Mara's limbs to the bed and glued her eyelids shut was immune to the nurses who flung open the unlocked doors and roused patients from their drug-induced nightmares. Rarely had she been so overcome with fatigue that even cutting was an act beyond her capabilities, but her fingers could not have closed around the precious shard of glass no matter how badly she craved her endorphins. She had meant to ask the nurse something this morning. Or had she dreamt it? She could barely tell the difference anymore.

In the cafeteria, she nearly dozed off into a plate of powdery scrambled eggs, and during group therapy forced her eyes to stay open despite the endless drone of the doctor's voice, the same doctor who could not carve out five minutes of his ever-so-important schedule to evaluate her in private. Now she sat in the dayroom, a far greater punishment than confinement to one's room. Most of the patients directed their pharmaceutical stares at one of the handful of channels allowed on the obsolete CRT television mounted in the corner. Cathode rays bombarded the viewers, and in return, they lobbed their psychic, psychotic energies back at the screen. It would explain most reality TV, and if there were any truth to memetic engineering, it rationalized the sheer number of people admitted to wards like this in the first place. Some muttered to themselves, or sat in stone-faced silence on the sofa. Some twitched and grimaced in the throes of irreversible tardive dyskinesia brought about by the very medication designed to force normality upon them. Mara found an empty chair next to an older man in a wheelchair. Gray peppered his otherwise black hair, especially at the temples, and unlike the rest of the zombies here, something resembling life still glimmered in his dark eyes.

He was one of the patients that did not speak, and Mara didn't blame him. What could you talk about with people who thought the staff had planted tiny microphones in the breakfast potatoes so they could listen to the secret messages encoded in peristalsis? She scanned the distressingly sunny room for her roommate and blinked against the glare. No sign of her. Mara didn't recall seeing her when she woke up, either, though she'd been barely conscious. Had she died in the night? Did they zip her into a body bag with Mara sleeping three feet away?

The hands of the round clock on the wall hadn't moved since she sat down, though the second hand juddered back and forth, undecided if time should march forward.

Something about the man beside her reminded

Mara of her grandfather. He appeared to be of Asian descent, and it bothered her. She began to rise so she could find another spot, one close to the door perhaps, but the man shot out his arm and seized her wrist.

"Sit."

Mara lowered herself back into the chair without argument. The man did not speak again for what seemed like hours. Then:

"I know why you're here."

"No offense, but that's not hard to figure out."

"It's that woman."

"What… woman?" Mara asked, but her heart had already quickened its pace in anticipation of the answer.

"You see them, don't you? The dead. But no one believes you. That's why you're here."

An icy river like the one in the forest threaded through Mara's chest.

"You don't know what's real and what isn't anymore. But they're real, and they're calling you. It's why you want to sleep all the time. It's when your mind is most open to them, when they can slip in and use your electromagnetic impulses to manifest."

"Who are you? How do you know this?"

"Okubo, Mara," the head nurse called from the doorway. Mara leapt at least six inches out of the chair. "Time for your individual therapy session."

"Find me again tomorrow," the man whispered.

"I can tell you everything."

Mara gazed down at him, unable to formulate the words she so urgently needed to speak. The nurse tapped the sole of her sensible white shoe against the floor.

"Okubo!"

"Tomorrow," Mara agreed, and rushed to the door.

She hadn't even been evaluated yet, so "therapy" consisted of a series of vague questions asked by a doctor—not *the* doctor, of course; he was too busy organizing group sessions and avoiding her at all costs—apparently designed to keep her here as long as possible.

She yawned frequently, and her head drooped against her chest. The doctor sighed, scribbled something in her file, and dismissed her. When she fell asleep at dinner onto an overcooked pork chop impractical to cut with plastic utensils, the nurse finally ushered her to her room. The back wall where her absentee roommate had slept opened onto a forest, a black river shimmering with tiny lights, summoning her forward to find that impossible house. This time she must enter it.

\* \* \*

The nurse all but dragged Mara to the dayroom the next morning, after failing to rouse her for breakfast or group despite her prodding and shouting. That

Mara couldn't remember her dreams disturbed her, which gave her even more motivation to do nothing but sleep. He called to her, even when she was awake. A hushed voice inside her brain, beckoning her like a lullaby into slumber. *Hush-a-bye, don't you cry, go to sleep little baby...*

It was the damned drugs. She must start hiding the pills under her tongue. Mustn't let them inject her with anything. Must behave. She could sleep without them.

She sat in the same chair beside the man as she had the day before, and waited for him to speak.

"For years you've known it's all wrong. Sometimes you feel like you're slipping out of your own life."

*That's exactly what I called it. Slipping.*

"You see things, hear things, no one else does. And then, at the house, something happened to you. It sits over a powerful conduit—an underground river—and they flocked to you. When you woke up, the world was different. Like an inescapable nightmare. You know how it's supposed to be, and yet you can't find the way back. This is what happened to me, too.

"The first law of thermodynamics states that energy is never created or destroyed; it can only be transformed. When we die, what happens to our bioelectric currents? If they cannot be destroyed, what do they become?"

How did he know these questions she had asked

herself a thousand times? Had he read her journals somehow?

"It turns out that *we* are their conduits. I don't know what will close the gateway between the living and the dead now."

"What gateway? I don't understand. How do you know all these things about me?" A bubble of nausea rose in Mara's throat. She didn't belong here. Not with strange men who could look into her heart and read the torments inscribed upon it.

"The spirits feed on your agony, just as they feed on mine. It's the only thing that makes you feel alive, after all, isn't it? That suffering? And that is what they want, more than anything. To feel alive. Radios, televisions, phones… dreams …if it uses electrical energy to function, they can find a pathway through it. You carried them inside, and they've found the way out." His stare burned into her; he could have peeled away her charred flesh and read her entrails. "They'll have you now. They know the darkness in your soul, and they will use it to break you. They know what you fear most. You crossed the river, and now you're trapped between two worlds."

"What does that *mean*?"

He tugged down the front of his gown. Mara glanced at the nurses, who chatted by the windows. Not looking. Not caring. A latticework of crimson gouges spread like the branches of a dead tree across his chest, stretching toward his neck as if to strangle him with their spindly fingers. She thought of her roommate. Still no sign of her.

"You asked for death, each time you cut yourself. She answered. Why else did you cut, except to take away pain? Even if it was just your own." He settled back into his chair and sealed his lips together like a freezer bag, as though he'd never spoken at all.

"Who *are* you?" Mara demanded, but the man might as well have been a wax statue in Madame Tussauds.

When the patients lined up to be shepherded to the dining hall, he was the first to leave the dayroom. Mara spotted him near the door, picking at overcooked rotini drowned by a sauce that resembled tomatoes in color only.

She never saw him again.

\* \* \*

She wondered, when she returned to her room after dinner and found the red, leather-bound book lying on the floor, if he had slipped it under the door knowing his time here had ended. Mara crawled into her bed and tugged the covers over the book in case one of the nurses barged in. Her new roommate, currently enduring intake, ought to arrive shortly. She had to make the most of her brief solitude. Mara unlatched the journal as if handling a priceless antique and flipped to the last two written pages, which bore a disconcerting resemblance to her own handwriting.

*According to quantum mechanics, objective reality does not even exist. Descartes once wrote, "There is never any reliable way of distinguishing being awake from being asleep." Our senses cannot be trusted; they are easily deceived. But our minds do not exist in a physical space, and so reality is only what we perceive it to be. There are as many worlds as there are people, but what of those created by people no longer living? Do these worlds simply disappear when the body expires? Or, because the mind is a nonphysical entity, do they persist in some form, just like our bioelectrical energy? Are dreams the portal into their dimension, and vice-versa? Are we in this hospital merely because reality is, in fact, subjective? Who are these doctors to say the things I see aren't real? How are they to know if any of us are real? They do not understand that, if the dead have their way, theirs will be the only reality left. Because if one cannot reliably distinguish between sleeping and waking, one cannot reliably distinguish between being alive and being dead.*

"This is crazy," Mara whispered. She knew virtually nothing of quantum mechanics or philosophy. She looked up into the corners of the room for cameras. Spying on her, they *must* be—

This place was really getting to her. Infecting her.

*Dreams are the portal, and her mansion of the soul is as haunted as any abandoned house in the woods. And the girl remembers the day the dead found her in a waking nightmare, the day she was chosen. She remembers her grandfather's tales of the Yomi, the subterranean land of the dead through which flows a dark river...*

Mara slammed the book shut and stuffed it into the space between the bed and the nightstand. Her entire body quivered with the weight of knowledge she did not want. Subjective actuality. None of this was real. Or all of it was real. Or it was someone else's reality. A headache split her skull down the middle. This, she thought, was what they meant by "cracking up." And yet the concept made a terrifying sort of sense, though every instinct railed against it.

She was lost, and she did not know how to get home.

\* \* \*

Mara saw her old roommate that night, one last time, walking through a wall. She left behind a black smudge on the paint.

\* \* \*

Her journal. That was what she had meant to ask the nurse. She had to sign for it; the indignity of having to request her own property, for a bound stack of paper, at that—what harm could she inflict? Death by paper cut?—was grotesque. She had to promise to return it by the end of the day, or they would permanently confiscate it. If the insanity here had turned contagious, then dehumanizing events like this served as its vector of transmission. One could not observe a system without changing it.

Mara sat in the craft room with the only writing utensil allowed to her. Not a pen, not even a pencil, but a fat, harmless black crayon. Dull and waxy and barely legible along the college-ruled lines of her journal. The other journal remained hidden in her room. She had figured out where they checked, and when, and moved it accordingly.

Some of the patients finger-painted or scribbled with crayons on construction paper. Every bit the children the staff considered them to be, infantilized more for the damage they might perpetrate upon the nurses than for their own safety. Still, the craft room allowed a degree of self-expression, though even those crude drawings would be analyzed in due time for any hint that the meds needed adjustment. Mara found an empty table in the back of the room, hunched her shoulders, and pulled her hair down into her face to ward off any would-be gestures of friendship.

*Heisenberg,* she wrote, *said, "We have to remember that what we observe is not nature in itself but nature exposed to our method of questioning." No objective reality. Most people experience quantum decoherence and cannot detect the other worlds that exist all around them. I, however, live in a world dreamed up by people who aren't even alive anymore.*

These words… they could not be hers. She examined the tip of the crayon as if it would impart to her who commanded it to write things she did not understand. That, of course, was akin to checking the corners for spy cameras.

*They are as real as I am, because I cannot prove that I am real at all.*

\* \* \*

In the forest's perpetual darkness, the wind carried whispers that might have been the rustle of pine needles, or the voices of those whom the wood had spirited away. Mara opened her eyes. She stood upon the broken flagstone walkway as snow, wet but peculiarly not cold, fluttered down against her cheeks, nose, and eyelids.

The house had grown. An implausibility, yet more stories stacked themselves atop the existing structure, and more wings sprang from it like a mechanical insect unfolding its legs. In the courtyard, below the headless statue, a little girl spread her arms and legs and waved them up and down through the snow until an angel took shape beneath her. She sat up and focused her dark eyes on Mara. Her mouth moved with words to which Mara was deaf. The girl embraced the statue, her eyes closed and her lips turned up in a red crescent like a lunar eclipse. Then she lay back down, smiling, as the snow floated down until only a nebulous human shape remained. After a few minutes, even that vanished under a mantle of white.

And there was Jason, light as the snow itself as he walked over it. With each step, a crimson rose sprouted from the lifeless earth. He ascended the steps and pulled open the front door.

This time Mara followed him.

# CONDUITS

The House had metamorphosed on the inside as much as the outside. Where in the forest house at the base of the mountain Mara had found large, Western-style rooms, here were long hallways with sliding wooden doors, exposed rafters, and tatami mats for floors. An American girl through and through, she found Japanese architecture oppressive and frightening, particularly in a place that so resembled her grandfather's house. Claustrophobia pressed against her limbs, worked its extremities into her lungs.

Most of the structure existed in darkness, yet in some places lanterns hung suspended from chains attached to the ceiling, or tea light candles burned on decrepit side tables as if to guide her. Many of the rooms were altar rooms, with *kamidana* set high into the far walls so no one could pass under them, and offerings of rice and flowers left to the chosen spirit. In the shrines were mirrors and *shinzō* sculptures, the *shintai* through which the spirits took physical form. Paper *o-fuda* inscribed with the name of one *kami* or another—Mara had never bothered to learn the entirely too complex Japanese writing system—hung from doors and ceilings as protective amulets. She avoided the mirrors, fearing the spirits she might see there would not be the benevolent *kami*.

Labyrinthine halls twisted this way and that. Many of the doors were jammed, swollen shut from cycles of heat and moisture, but behind some, rose screams that rivaled those in the deepest pits of hell. What house did Jason see? One filled with light and happy memories or, like this, built upon the bones of sorrow and self-loathing? And she had built it, of that she was now certain. Everything since her sister's death, even Jason, a self-inflicted punishment inviting misery. Bars on her soul, imprisoning herself.

Mara tugged at the next door. It opened, like so much of the house, into darkness. When her eyes adjusted, she could make out boxes stacked in the corners, much like the house in what she'd believed to be the real world, and furniture still wrapped in plastic. The odor of rodent droppings, mold, and effluvia of countless accumulated eras burned in her nostrils. A large oval mirror, not a *shintai* but the kind made expressly for human vanity, hung on a wall behind a rotted, moth-eaten dressing screen. The screen must have been beautiful once, painted with cherry blossoms and snowy mountain peaks, natural *shintai*. Mara trailed her fingertips over it as she approached the mirror, cobwebs from the low rafters clinging to her skin. Hollows where her eyes should be. Hair like a dark veil behind which to hide herself, stringy and speckled with dust and residue. Her flesh merely smoke that would dissipate if anyone touched it. She had seen a face like this before, somewhere…

And over her shoulder another face, the same hollow eyes and dark hair, the lips purple from lack of oxygen. Those lips moving in a silent plea Mara did not understand.

"I know you," Mara whispered, though it wasn't possible.

Behind her in the hallway, the floorboards creaked. Something scratched against the ancient wood as it slithered across the floor.

*When you hear the singing,* said a voice, but the face in the mirror was gone, *you will know it is time.*

The scratching louder now, something sharp scoring the wood. Mara held her breath. Silence stabbed her eardrums like ice picks, and a cold from beneath the floor flowed over her until she froze in place. A hiss of static, then a crackling like flame, an errant transmission lost in the ether of space and time:

> *When I was little, little, little,*
> *I played, played, played,*
> *When I was oldie, oldie, oldie,*

*I was sick, sick, sick,*
*And when I was dead, dead, dead,*
*I was scared, scared, scared.*

Mara gasped; in the hush, the sound roared like a jet engine. The tick of her heart tapped out a message to whatever lurked in the hallway.

*Scrape… scrape… scrape…*

She turned ever so slowly, not allowing herself to look at the door she wished she had closed behind her, and spied another doorway on the far end of the room. It might be a closet. A dead end. A stairway to nowhere.

She ran.

\* \* \*

"…did you give her? This is not a normal sleeping pattern, even for someone on antipsychotics."

"We haven't given her anything not approved by the unit doctor—"

"I'll be having a chat with him this afternoon. And how is she getting out of the room and into others every night when she sleepwalks?"

"The doors are all locked, Doctor, and there's nothing on the cameras—"

"But multiple patients claim to see her in their rooms, and several orderlies have verified she's missing when they do their rounds. Have you got an answer for that?"

Apparently, the nurse did not.

"Ms. Okubo, it's time to wake up."

Hands prodding her, but not the rough and careworn hands of the nurses. Her savior. He had found her lost in the wood and brought her back to the real world. If she could unseal this glue on her eyelids, if she could speak to the doctor, the actual doctor at last, he'd set everything right.

"Easy, now. It's all right." Pills stuffed into her mouth. Water dribbled down her chin and onto her gown. "These will help you wake up."

*Scrape... scrape... scrape...*

A stunted scream escaped Mara's lips. She glanced around the room, her heart filled with helium and rising into her throat. Dark hair dangled from the ceiling, and hands reached from the floor, swaying like anemones as they sought to grasp—

The doctor hooked a hand under her arm and helped her stand up. "My office isn't far."

Her feet barely moved as he led her down the hall. The lights were too bright, the ward too loud with incoherent screaming, nurses chattering at their station, the overwhelming racket of a world to which she no longer belonged. Her brain shrieked for relief.

She slumped into a chair not unlike the one she remembered from her principal's office so long ago —the distraught man hadn't a clue what else to do with her until the police came—across from the doctor's desk. She had to go back. Find Jason and atone for her failure. Fix the rift that had stolen reality from her. She was not one of them. One cut, just one, and she could assure herself of it…

"I'm very concerned about your lethargy, Ms. Okubo. The pills tend to make patients sleepy, but not at the level you're exhibiting. Can you tell me what's wrong?"

"The house…"

He furrowed his brow and scribbled something on a yellow legal pad. "Tell me about the house."

"It… changes." Each word was a Sisyphean effort. "And he's… in there."

"Your boyfriend."

She managed half a nod.

"What about your sister? Is she in the house, too?"

"I don't know. There's something in the dark…"

"Tell me about her."

"Why?"

"You refused to talk about her when you were in Harborview. I think it's time. Tell me what happened, Mara. You're safe now, and no one is here to judge you."

But that was a lie, wasn't it? She was here precisely because society had judged her unfit to participate in it. Mara wanted to crawl inside herself where no one could find her. "Please," she whispered, but he kept picking at her scabs.

"What happened that day? Do you remember?"

"I… I found her."

"What happened before that?"

"Please…" Mara drew up her knees and squeezed them to her chest, willing herself to disappear. Her hands trembled, an addict desperate for a fix. A razor blade, a utility knife…

A shard of glass…

*I'm sorry,* she had said, over and over. The cops wanted to feel disgust but gazed at her with pity, as she wept until she ran out of breath, until her eyes swelled so much she could barely open them. She refused the food they offered her. She did not deserve such amenities. A short time later, the court sentenced her to five years at Harborview. She was thirteen.

She had finished high school in a mental hospital. When she emerged that summer, all her friends had long since forsaken her, denied that she had ever held even a modicum of significance in their lives. In that sense, she supposed, reality *was* subjective. She was the rumor freshmen whispered about, the boogeyman that haunted the corridors after hours. Her only salvation lay in the court sealing her record due to her age, so that every Ivy League school to which she applied accepted her into their Writing or Communications programs. She could start over, and no one had to know her horror story.

But she barely remembered; that was the worst part. She had found her sister in an empty classroom, and then returned to her own class in bloody clothes. No, that wasn't quite right. She had been in the classroom with her all along. The sliver of glass from the broken window gripped in her hand as if it had become a part of her. Her palm bled, though she did not feel the glass carve into the meat of her hand. Blood spraying from her sister's throat like a lawn sprinkler. No one ever taught that in biology class, what arteries did when severed.

Mara scratched her thigh. Last night, before she fell asleep, she had gathered the courage to lift her gown as high as her breasts. The slashes deep and red, from her thigh all the way to her abdomen, conformed to the contours of her ribs. The terrible darkness inside her clawing or slicing its way out, as though her dreams had made it a tangible entity. She felt it drawing fingernails or glass across her skin. The rose was all but lost in a dense, inflamed tangle of lacerations.

"It was like she wasn't even there," she said. She twisted the hem of the gown. "Because she was already dead to me."

"What do you mean by that?"

"I had to make the sacrifice. I was chosen, but I got it wrong."

As if by magic, Mara had found the glass in her hand. She could not recall breaking the window, or if it had been damaged by a stray baseball, perhaps even by vandals. Mara slashed at the arms that fought to defend against her attack, gouging long scarlet valleys into Joby's flesh. Unpopular, scrawny, bullied Joby, for whom Mara felt the most unendurable pity. *Now you will be remembered forever,* she had thought, *and in death, they will love you. I do this because I love you.* She had ripped the blade across Joby's throat. Had said nothing during the assault; the glass spoke every word she might have uttered.

He leaned forward, his eyes sharp as stars. "Why?"

"I wanted to take her pain, but I wasn't strong enough. I was carrying too much of my own."

The doctor's ballpoint raced across his yellow legal pad. Had he told her his name? She couldn't remember. When he set down the pen, he took a long sip of coffee from which steam had ceased to rise, curled his lip, and pushed the Styrofoam cup aside. "You expressed a great deal of remorse for what happened. The death of your boyfriend has obviously triggered feelings of guilt that are manifesting through your current symptoms. Do you believe you deserve to be punished?"

So many doors to the past, and she had walked through the one that never closed. Her parents wanted to ship her off to Japan, not because of Jason, but because they looked at her, who had shamed them with her madness, and saw their dead eldest daughter. Better they'd never had children at all. Better to forget they had. What sort of immortality was this?

"I thought it was him," she said softly, and her voice sounded like someone else's, a stranger's. "But she had to use him to get to me. To open the portal. She's the one who lured me in. She wants revenge. And why shouldn't she? It was supposed to be me all along. I was supposed to kill myself. *I* was the sacrifice. I would have spared them all so much pain… and myself."

"What is the portal you mentioned just now? Do you mean your dreams?"

"'We live on a placid island of ignorance in the midst of black seas of infinity, and it was not meant that we should voyage far.' H. P. Lovecraft said that. But I have voyaged. I've gone… somewhere, and now I can't get back. Don't you ever have the feeling, even just for a second, that you're in the wrong place? The wrong… world?" She needed confirmation, no matter how small. Something to truss her to the realm of the living, even if he only admitted to the intrusive thoughts everyone experienced now and then. The dead, always having but one purpose, would never confess to such a thing.

The doctor set his pen down and, bowing his head, steepled his fingers together. Exasperated with her, perhaps, though he had surely seen patients much farther gone than she was. Hadn't he?

"What you're describing is called 'derealization,' and it's common in a number of disorders. There's an abnormality in the way you experience or observe the world beyond yourself, and now it seems unreal to you. Sometimes this develops after a traumatic event. It's also common in lucid dreaming, which I understand is a frequent occurrence for you. However, based on your history and what we've observed here, I am concerned that we're dealing with primary depersonalization disorder. So." More notes in illegible doctor-scrawl. "We can start you on clonazepam, and if you don't respond to that, we'll try lamotrigine—"

"According to quantum mechanics, objective reality doesn't even exist. But Descartes figured that out in the seventeenth century. Was he locked away? Should quantum physicists take lamotrigine? There is a deviation in my perception because *this isn't my world*." She drew up her knees and curled her arms around them. Tears stung her eyes. "I don't know if I'm awake or asleep. I don't know if I'm alive or dead. And neither do you. Either way, we're all just electrical impulses."

"Mara…" The doctor rubbed his temples. He didn't understand. Didn't *want* to understand. She could not fault him for refusing to accept that everything he thought was real was, in fact, merely his mind's opinion on the matter. "She can't forgive you if you can't forgive yourself."

"Then…" Mara's eyelids drooped with the familiar lassitude that called her home. "She never will."

\* \* \*

Lanterns burned at each end of the hall, where smoke-like smudges resembling human shadows blackened the walls. *This is what I'll be in the morning.* A ghost of a memory. Like her roommate, or the man in the wheelchair, whose names she could not remember or had never known in the first place. If they had existed at all.

The air was warm, stale, crowded with souls and with sorrow. From around the corner, where the light did not reach, came the sound:

*Scrape… scrape… scrape…*

*I don't know what will close the gateway between the living and the dead.*

The solution had become increasingly obvious. Close the channel. But there was, of course, only one way to do that.

Tendrils slinked around Mara's throat. She stopped beside the lantern, not wanting to go further even if it meant seeing Jason, not ready to face the thing in the darkness. To close the channel.

*Down below,* whispered the walls, *the river runs red with our blood.*

"Is that what you want? Another sacrifice?"

*Only one who is willing can end our pain.*

"Willing to do what? I'm here, aren't I?"

*You do not know how we suffered. How your sister suffered. Are you prepared to know?*

The suggestion that she could do anything for them made her sound heroic, and she was nothing of the sort.

*If not, then we will continue to call out to our loved ones. They have what we most wish for. We will call out, then they will call out, and onward it will spread until there is no one left living. Then our envy finally will be as dead as we are.*

"What will happen to them all? There are so many ghosts."

*Most are only residual energy. A memory replaying itself over and over. They have no awareness, no intelligence. They will remain. Only we are the ones who hunger, who know that we are dead, and why.*

*Lie down, Mara,* said the darkness, *and dream.*

"But... I *am* dreaming. Aren't I?" She had no idea, no frame of reference. The border between dream and reality was so porous that she never fully belonged to one or the other anymore, but to both all at once.

Somewhere down the hall, a door grated open. Reluctant to leave the lantern's safety, Mara scurried toward the sound and darted into an open room, then pushed the door shut behind her. A mattress lay in one corner. Above it, a straw doll in bloody clothes, with black hairs woven into the chaff, was skewered into the wall.

"Who is it?" she whispered. She had seen such a thing before. Grandpa had lived in a village at the foot of Mount Hayachine, which he called Adzumanedake in the ancient tongue. A *shintai*, like so many of the mountains. His village clung to the antiquated rituals in ever-smaller numbers, while the rest of the country modernized around them, but a straw doll wearing Grandma's kimono had sat at the local shrine for a month after she died.

*You already know the answer.*

Mara lay on the mattress, beneath a curtained window illuminated by a blue-white moon she could not see. Across from her, an *okiagari-koboshi* doll bobbed and swayed as if pushed by an unseen child. The legless, bottom-weighted doll glared at her with painted eyes.

"And when I was dead, dead, dead," she sang, her voice fading into oblivion, becoming one with it, "I was scared, scared, scared."

The door opened.

\* \* \*

"There are many stories to tell," said Grandpa, who seemed to enjoy few things more than frightening his young grandchildren. Perhaps that was not his intent at all but merely the nature of their folklore, an innately terrifying mythology of ghosts, demons, and murder. "Shall I tell you of the *Jukai* to the south, at the foot of the most sacred mountain? A forest haunted by the dead."

"Dad," Mom protested, "I'll never get her to sleep tonight."

"She should know the legends of her people. You move to America and have children, give them American names, and they grow up knowing nothing of their culture."

Mom chuckled and patted his shoulder in that good-natured but dismissive way the young often expressed toward the old, before leaving the room to make tea.

"Now we use dolls and other things to appease the gods. But once upon a time, they were not so easy to please. Perhaps that is why they have forgotten us, because we have not honored them as we should." A faraway look descended over Grandpa's dark eyes.

"Tell me about the *miko*," Mara said.

With a deep sigh, Grandpa seemed to return to himself. If only a little. "Little girls always want stories of maidens, don't they? Very well. Once there lived in the mountains a *horimono miko*…"

\* \* \*

They brought her nothing but sadness—a lost love, a death in the family. Why would they bring her anything else? Happiness was an emotion they wanted to keep. And it was her duty, after all, to take their sorrows into herself, for all they had done for her, clothing her and feeding her and leaving offerings to the god whom she served. She loved them well, as she might have loved her own children were she not called to such a sacred obligation. And like any parent, she desired nothing more than to protect her brood.

She made her home in Adzumanedake, a *miko*

within the shrine, and each day one or two villagers ascended the mountain path to seek her counsel. *How can I help them?* she wondered. Then she conceived the idea to make of her own body an offering to the gods. She began the *bokukei* upon herself so her people would no longer feel the pain in their own souls, for she was an instrument of the gods. After each story, she engraved her flesh with a shard of glass, each *horimono* upon her skin a punishment for failing as the village's protector to appease the gods who allowed such suffering. She carved and she carved, until her blood stained her skin red, and not a single inch remained free from an inscription of suffering and loss. The villagers began to fear her, for her appearance grew more terrifying than any *oni*, though her spirit remained as kind and gentle as ever. She prayed for the gods to read the story of her flesh and free her of her affliction, for the villagers' sorrows had grown too heavy to bear. But the gods remained silent, and fewer and fewer villagers made the pilgrimage to her sanctuary, until she sat alone in her shrine and wept in isolation.

The human body can endure only so much, especially from such carvings as she withstood. The agony became so great that, after a time, no one could rouse her from sleep. As she lay upon her mattress, the dead whose memories dwelled in each *horimono* claimed her as their own. Before she fell into eternal sleep, however, she placed two slivers of glass in her eyes, the only part of her yet unmarked. That very morning a brave girl had made the climb in a quest to rid herself of the burden that her lost love imposed upon her. She did not think the *horimono miko* fearsome; on the contrary, she discovered a deific beauty in the pattern of scars carved into her naked flesh. And so, in the glass, the *miko*'s ruined eyes reflected the final pain she accepted, of a girl who had assuaged her loneliness in her dying moments, a girl who herself had been abandoned by the one she loved.

\* \* \*

"But why, Grandpa? Why would she want to take their pain?"

"Because through suffering, we become purified. And to suffer for another human being is the noblest thing we can do."

The shrine festivals had begun that week, and Grandpa took them to see the *Kagura* at a stage near the mountain. A black screen dyed with the temple's name in the center divided the platform, and a drummer sat facing it with a cymbalist on either side of him. All wore white kimonos. Flutes and voices rose from behind the partition. Bored and cold, wiping her nose on the sleeve of her coat when her nose began to run, Mara let her mind wander for much of the performance—until the manic *Fuhsho* dance. The dancers wore horsehair wigs in black, white, and brown, and masks in which the god lived so that they became avatars of him until the end, when they pulled them off and resumed their human forms. How glorious it must be to become a vessel of the divine, even for a few minutes. An honor to be chosen, an honor she would never receive, born and living in America. She thought sometimes that her mother was embarrassed to have grown up in such a superstitious place as this.

Mara looked over at the shrine, just across a small river whose source lay somewhere in the mountain, at the red *torii* gates looming above the path. Something drew her gaze up the steps. Despite the gloom shading the *haiden*, where the public worshipped, Mara distinguished the shape of a woman, whose naked breasts and hips revealed *horimono* etchings so deep they had blackened with dried blood. Her entire body was shorn of hair, her scalp and even her most intimate parts inscribed with the torments of others, and her mouth was moving. Mara couldn't possibly hear her from that distance, yet she did, as clearly as if they stood beside each other. The voice was one of immense pain, so mournful that it brought tears to Mara's eyes. It scratched its way into her ears:

*When the time comes, will you make the sacrifice? Will you do what you must to end our suffering, and yours?*

And when Mara saw the glass in her eyes, and even from such a distance saw herself reflected in it, she began to weep.

\* \* \*

In Grandpa's house, Mara and Joby slept in the same room, on small twin beds at least as old as Grandpa. They squeaked whenever one of them turned over, and the springs dug into Mara's side through the thin mattress. There was no box spring. Joby nevertheless fell asleep within minutes, as she always did, but Mara lay awake and stared at the ceiling. It was strange here, so quiet, not like Seattle at all. No street traffic, no lights from outside, just silence grinding through the house. Like being on another planet.

She hated it.

Joby snored peacefully on the other side of the tiny room. Mara shifted her gaze to the door, which slid open like the doors to their patio instead of swinging open and shut like normal doors. Nothing here was normal.

A shadow materialized on the door. There was no light outside to cast such a shape, or any shape, upon the wood, and Mara felt the strange sense of slipping out of her own life as she often did when she cut. She had begun cutting two years ago already, and if anyone suspected, they'd never spoken a word of it. If they ignored the issue, perhaps it would go away. Like the shadow.

But the shadow did not go away. It only

solidified, became the thing Mara prayed it would not, the thing she hoped she had only imagined after the excitement of the *Fuhsho*.

The woman with glass in her eyes.

The carvings in her skin, black with ancient dried blood, the crude drawings and *kanji*, rippled with a life of their own, eager to tell their stories anew. Mara swallowed her scream. She didn't want to wake Joby, or her parents. Or especially Grandpa.

The *miko* stood over the bed and peered down at her, though she could surely see nothing. The slivers of glass punctured straight through her pupils, and her eyeballs had shriveled up in their sockets, leaving a faint sheen of dried retinal fluid over the etchings on her cheeks. She reached out one hand. Mara held her breath and drew up her knees as she tugged the blanket up over her nose.

The blanket peeled away. Defenseless, Mara could do nothing but squeeze her eyes shut as the cold, dead fingers examined her thighs and inner arms exposed by the seasonally inappropriate pajamas she wore. They traced each pallid scar, scars that had faded quickly because Mara hadn't yet gathered the courage to cut deeper.

*Your wounds speak to me.*

Mara blinked. Her tongue clicked dryly in her mouth.

*They want what you do not. Make the sacrifice. We will not rest unless you help us.*

Mara's mouth opened in a soundless scream.

The *miko* leaned even closer to her, closer, until the distance between their bodies closed and a shocking chill like the cold of space itself filled each molecule of Mara's body. The last thing she saw was the shards of glass in the *miko*'s eyes, prisms in which her own mutilated face stared back at her.

\* \* \*

Mara breathed deeply. The suffocating silence enclosed her like a coffin.

Joby was there, on the floor. The scratching sound came from her fake nails digging into the wood. She had tried to crawl out of the classroom, they said, but died within a minute of Mara's leaving. Her head twisted up, exposing the yawning gash in her throat and the dried blood splattered on her face, down her shirt, striping her arms. This was the reality of what Mara had done, confronting her at last with its mindless brutality. Her sister—once her best friend, her playmate and confidante. It had gone wrong after Japan, somehow, in the intervening years after Grandpa's death. She did not belong to herself anymore. And Joby, slow to mature, underdeveloped and bookish, the butt of cruel jokes and pranks. The first pain engraved on Mara's heart, through which she had learned to view her entire life as an endless valley of loneliness. Only the ghosts ever stayed with her.

"I'm so sorry, Joby. I'm so sorry." Like that day in

the police station, a mantra without meaning. An empty apology, the words as weightless as air.

*We're waiting for you in the basement. When it's over, we'll sleep forever. And so will she.*

She flickered and went out, leaving a formless dark stain on the floor. The *okiagari-koboshi* doll stopped rocking. Mara returned to the hallway and pursued the faint tinkling of bells, the flitting of orbs like fireflies dancing in the dark. The echoes of the dead whispered in a spectral wind through the twisting hallways, their torture imprinted on the walls, formed into molecules in the air.

Turns, and more turns. A maze of corridors leading into the heart of the house, and this time Mara knew she would not find her way out. She'd known since the Kagura she *had* been chosen, but for something she could not have comprehended as a child. To prevent the world from becoming the graveyard she carried in her soul.

Ahead of her, ephemeral figures trudged in solemn procession down the longest corridor of all. Unseen drummers tapped out a pattern to ward off evil and, matching their rhythm, the cavalcade scattered salt left, then right. All wore hideous *yokai* masks that erased their identities.

*You don't know, do you? No one ever told you. When the* horimono miko *died, a terrible plague fell upon the village. The villagers decided there was only one thing left to do— make a sacrifice to the mountain. They sacrificed all the virgin children to purify the village.*

*But this ritual offended the gods, and the dead refused to rest until a willing sacrifice went into the mountain. For centuries, death and disease haunted the village until one brave man climbed to the peak and, on the anniversary of her death, threw himself down.*

The casket had been closed... Mom always called it an "accident"...

*She took their pain and asked for nothing, and they would not even bring her down from the mountain because they were afraid. He did it for you, but it was too late. She had already found you.*

"There is glass," Mara said softly, "even in her eyes."

*You have been dead a very long time, Mara. You must cut. Give us rest. Save them all.*

How bad could that be, Mara thought, when cutting was all that reminded her she was real? Her tiny Rorschach blots, a pictorial of her life illustrated in blood. No other therapy had ever worked, and of course, the doctors in their failure had tried to take it from her. They wanted the violence against her own body to humiliate her, and so she told no one—not Andrea, not even Joby—except Jason. He understood, because he never felt alive, either. He welcomed death. He sought it out, teased it until it outwitted him at last. The bravest people, he said, were the ones who saw life for its futility and opted out of a game no one ever won. Funny, how people like him were called cowards.

The basement stairs groaned beneath her. Years

of tattered cobwebs dangled from the rafters, swept against her face and hair like murmurs. Water burbled in its secret language somewhere ahead, where the glimmering lantern light could not reach. The procession kept moving toward the sound, until one by one they melted away, twinkling with a golden light that floated off into the darkness.

Someone rinsed her face and hands with water, then waved a *haraegushi* wand over her body. The white papers feathered against her skin and she thought of flying away, the *haraegushi* as wings bearing her aloft into the purity of the sky. Frozen hands slipped her ankles into rope restraints. An unseen pulley creaked; she lost her balance and fell, but quickly rose upside down into the air, suspended over the river.

"I'm sorry, Joby," she said, her voice answering itself in echoes. Shapes squirmed on the floor below, like television static, like pale worms that writhed and moaned and reached for the fluid, the life, she promised to shed for them. The drums beat louder, and the cymbals crashed like her heartbeat in her ears.

The first cut was a bright flash of lightning across her thigh. Warm blood trickled up the inside of her leg and pattered against the wooden planks. The mouths beneath her yawned impossibly wide, necks craning and swollen purple tongues extended to receive their sacrament. The blade cut her other thigh. Invisible hands tore her clothes away, and cold air crawled over her with obscene intimacy. The ropes gnawed at the tender flesh inside her wrists. More slashes across her belly, breasts, and arms. Mara tensed and arched her back, the pain a violent red flare behind her eyes. The torment that festered within her rained upon them—Joby, Jason, Grandpa, the dead children of the village and those whom the *miko*'s wrath had claimed. The rope loosed her right hand and she found there a shard of glass, the missing part of her, and oh, how she wanted to cut it all out like gangrenous flesh. She did not hesitate before ripping the glass across her throat from one ear to the other, the gush of blood a roaring waterfall in her ears. Her smile tasted like blood.

Then the ropes went slack and she was falling toward the river, her pulse growing slower, fainter. Before she sank into endless, embracing darkness, she caught sight of Grandpa's withered face. And he wept tears of blood, for there was glass in his eyes.

\* \* \*

"What the hell kind of place is this, where patients can just walk out of here and no one notices?"

"Miss—"

"I brought her here so you could help her, not lose her!"

"Ms. Straub." The head nurse took a deep

breath and closed her eyes for half a second. Andrea had hoped for an outburst, more ammunition she could use in the lawsuit she fully intended to file. She'd already enlisted Nick to help her find a lawyer up to the task. "Ms. Okubo did not leave these premises. We've checked the security cameras, we've interviewed the guards—"

"So you're telling me what, she just… vanished? People don't do that!"

"Believe me, Ms. Straub, we are doing everything in our power to investigate this situation. We've already been in contact with the local authorities. But as of right now, we have no explanation." The nurse produced two small journals, the one Andrea recognized as Mara's, and another bound in red leather. "She kept the red journal hidden from us in her room. Were you aware of Ms. Okubo's interest in quantum physics and philosophy?"

"What? She's a magazine writer. Current events. She doesn't even like science." *Although,* Andrea thought, *she has an almost unhealthy interest in the paranormal, which only intensified after Jason's death.* But physics and the supernatural were opposite ends of the spectrum, one bolstered by scientific evidence and the other merely the product of a grieving mind. Andrea was no physics major herself, though she found the subject fascinating. To someone who didn't understand it at all, however, quantum theory and the paranormal could appear almost indistinguishable.

"It would seem there are many things no one knows about your friend. We need to keep the journals in case the police want to look at them, but I've made copies of the more… troubling pages for you. Maybe her parents can shed some light on what's in them. I'm very sorry, Ms. Straub. I understand that the last two months have been very difficult." The nurse handed to Andrea a sheaf of eleven-by-fourteen inch double-sided copies. Apparently, most of the journals' contents were troubling.

"It's okay for me to read these?"

"They are private journals and not part of her treatment, so they don't fall under HIPAA. I hope you won't mind if I give the police your contact information. You were closest to her, and I'm sure they'll want to talk to you."

They'd already written Mara off, and the cops probably had, too. Just another nut wandering the streets, no different from any other metropolitan area. She'd turn up on some street corner, like the crazy guy who tried to fly with the pigeons in the Straubs' old New York neighborhood. Mara wasn't their problem until she tried to hurt someone. But Mara had only ever wanted to hurt herself, and that didn't seem to matter to anyone.

Andrea folded the papers and tucked them into her shoulder bag. "Thanks."

"I'll make sure someone notifies you as soon as we have any news."

She nodded, but she expected no such phone call. The woman was telling her that her best friend of five years had vanished from a secure facility. What was the follow-up to that?

A guard stationed behind bulletproof glass buzzed her out of the ward and into the elevator lobby. Andrea's phone, set to vibrate, hummed inside her bag. She pulled it out. No bars, and instead of a signal the tiny white "Searching" icon spun endlessly around and around. The phone still purred, though it should have long since gone to voice mail.

She pressed "Answer" and held the phone to her ear.

Static. A crackle, a disembodied voice, like a radio tuner caught between stations. *Fucking prank callers.* She didn't need this right now.

"Hello? Answer me, asshole!"

"…all right… wanted…"

"Hello?" Her heart galloped upon recognizing the voice. "Mara? Mara!"

"…home now… don't worry…"

"Mara!"

The line went dead. Andrea, frantic, took half a step back toward the ward. She had to call someone, get help…

*Home now. Don't worry.*

She stared at the black screen of the phone still in her hand. Gradually her heartbeat slowed as a strange and sudden calm descended upon her. It was all right. Mara was all right.

Andrea rode the elevator down to the first-floor lobby. She smiled at the irritable information desk attendant, then opened the front doors onto a rare sunny Seattle afternoon. She retrieved the papers from her bag, tore them in half, and pitched them into the nearest trash receptacle.

All around her, people headed for the piers or Pike Place Market, the Space Needle, Pioneer Square. Only Andrea stood still, just for a moment, as the particles and molecules that were once Mara danced silently through her, like wind, and whispered that she had found herself.

# ABOUT THE AUTHOR

Jennifer Loring's short fiction has been published widely both online and in print, including the anthologies *Tales from the Lake vol. 1* and *vol. 4*, *Nightscript vol. 4*, and *Blood in the Rain vol. 4*. Longer work includes the novel *Those of My Kind* published by Omnium Gatherum. She holds an MFA in Writing Popular Fiction from Seton Hill University with a concentration in horror fiction and teaches online in SNHU's College of Continuing Education. Jenn lives with her husband in Philadelphia, PA, where they are owned by a turtle and two basset hounds. Find her online at http://jennifertloring.com.

www.ingramcontent.com/pod-product-compliance
Lightning Source LLC
Chambersburg PA
CBHW021025120726
47905CB00009B/3186